WHEN YOUR DRAGON IS TOO BIG FOR A BATH

AN ADVENTURE IN PRAYER

WRITTEN BY
C.E. WHITE

ILLUSTRATED BY
BHAGYA MADANASINGHE

When Your Dragon Is Too Big for a Bath by C.E. White

Illustrations by Bhagya Madanasinghe

Printed in the United States of America

ISBN 978-1-7332487-8-5

cewhitebooks@gmail.com
www.cewhitebooks.com
www.instagram.com/cewhitebooks
www.facebook.com/cewhitebooks

First Edition, November 2021

To God—who always gives me ideas and shows me what to do when things are too big for me.

I got a dragon for my birthday.
He was just an egg then.

I was so excited I nearly
dropped him!

My mom and dad said it was my job to take care of him. They gave me lots of books about dragons.

I read them all.

First, I had to put the egg under a lamp to keep it warm.
Dragons like it VERY warm.

It took a long... long... LONG time to hatch.

The egg finally started to rattle one day. It cracked down the middle, and out popped a shiny blue dragon with a purple tail!

I named him Wilfred.

We had lots of fun together!

All the dragon books said I had to give Wilfred a bath once a month, but he never liked baths.

During his first bath, he squirmed
and howled, but I could do it.
A dragon howl is pretty awful.

During his second bath,
he snorted and wiggled,
but I could still do it.

Things were going great!

Then Wilfred got bigger...

and bigger...

and **BIGGER!**

He started learning
to fly...oops!

I taught him that flying
was for outside.

He started making his
own dinner...yikes!

I taught him how to
use the toaster.

But when bath time came again, I couldn't teach him anything.

I tried pushing him in the water, but that didn't work.

I tried coaxing him into the
tub with his favorite treat.

I even tried bubbles, but Wilfred squirmed and howled and snorted and wiggled and refused to get in the water.

I couldn't do it.

Mom and Dad tried.
They couldn't do it either.

Wilfred was just too big.

My parents said when things get too big for them, they ask God for help. So we prayed.

I didn't think God was going to come give my dragon a bath, but I prayed anyway.

One week passed and then another.
Mom and Dad said if we couldn't figure out how to give
Wilfred a bath, he had to stay outside.

I could see why.
I could smell why, too.

But I didn't want him to stay outside. Wilfred kept my room warm at night and kept me company while I did my homework. He made me feel safe when I heard scary noises. He couldn't do that from outside.

So I prayed some more.

The next day, we were outside playing fetch when it started to rain. Wilfred didn't seem to mind the rain. He just kept flying after the ball.

And I got an idea!

I ran inside and grabbed the
soap and a towel.
When I came back out, Wilfred was waiting
for me to throw the ball again.

But he always loved a good belly scratch

...or back scratch

...or chin scratch.

He even let me scratch his feet,
but I think it must've tickled.

Before I knew it, Wilfred was clean all over.
But he was very soapy.

So we played fetch
some more, and the rain
rinsed him little by little.

We played
until the sun came out
and dried Wilfred off.

Mom and Dad were so
happy when they saw how
clean he was.

That night I asked them why God didn't answer my prayer.

"He did!" they said.

"But I'm the one who gave Wilfred a bath," I said. "It was my idea!"

"But who gave you the idea?" Mom asked.

"And who sent the rain?" Dad added.

"Yeah!" I said. "I guess God gave me the WAY to give Wilfred a bath!"

"Yes!" my mom said. "God doesn't always answer prayers the way we think He will or even the way we want."

"Like the time I prayed the lights would come back on in the storm because I was scared," I said. "They didn't come back on till the next day, but we had a fancy dinner with candles, and you taught me how to make shadow puppets with the flashlights. It was so fun, I wasn't scared anymore!"

"Exactly!" my mom said. "Instead of fixing the lights, God helped you to not be scared."

"I'm glad God does that kind of thing," Dad said, "because He knows exactly what's best for us even when we don't."

"Like when we were selling our old house," I said, "and I prayed we wouldn't have to move, but now I like it better here!"

Dad grinned. "I think you understand it better than I do!"

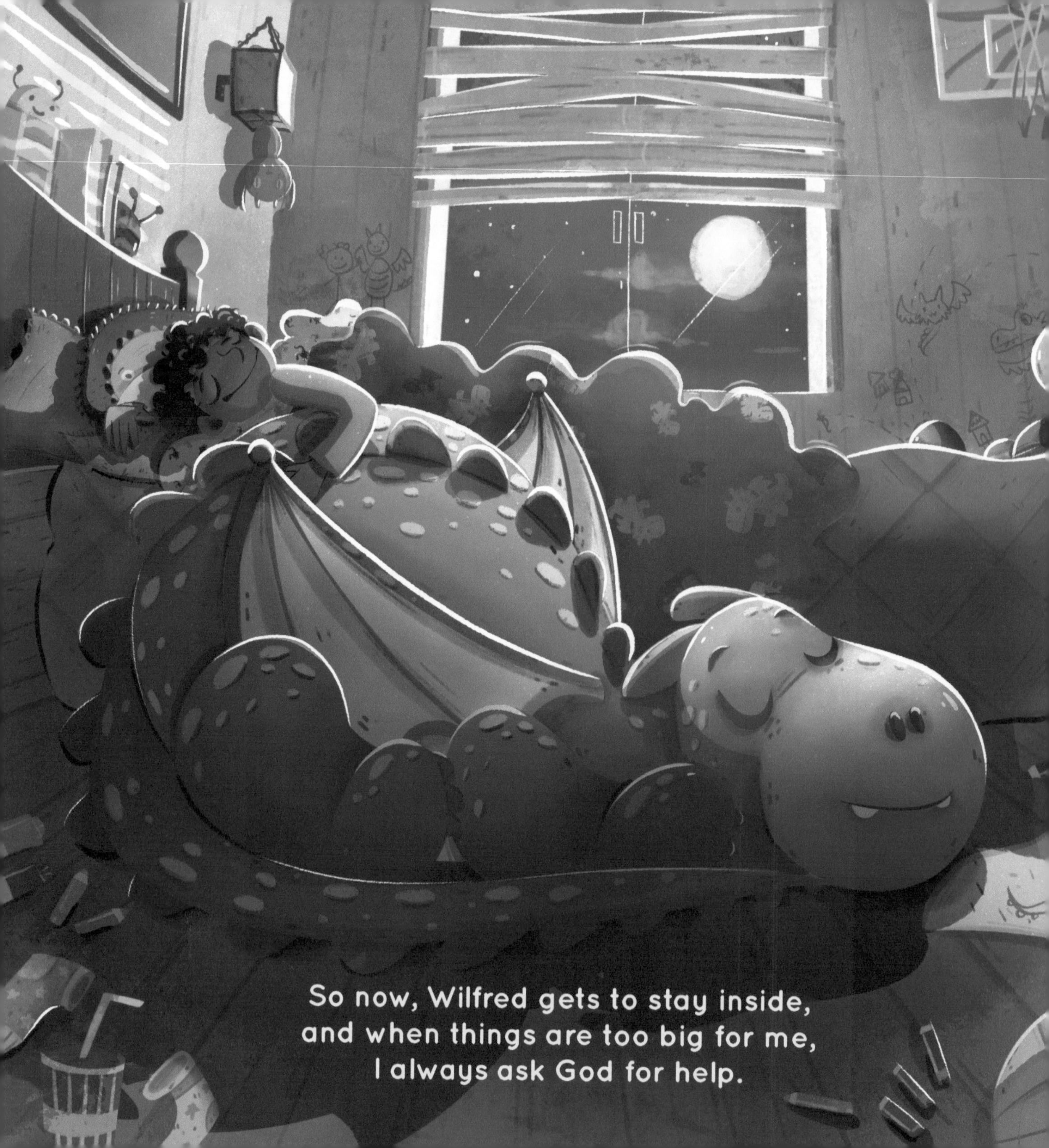

So now, Wilfred gets to stay inside,
and when things are too big for me,
I always ask God for help.

THE END

CPSIA information can be obtained
at www.ICGtesting.com
Printed in the USA
LVHW071915280222
712220LV00010B/610

* 9 7 8 1 7 3 3 2 4 8 7 8 5 *